Library of Congress Cataloging-in-Publication Data is available upon request.
ISBN 978-0-593-48484-5 (trade) — ISBN 978-0-593-48483-8 (lib. bdg.) • ISBN 978-0-593-48482-1 (ebook)
The artist used watercolor, gouache, and colored pencil to create the illustrations for this book. • The text of this book is set in 18-point Marion. • Interior design by Rachael Cole • MANUFACTURED IN CHINA
10 9 8 7 6 5 4 3 2 1 • First Edition

The artist would like to acknowledge the Herring Robes referenced on the "Remember you are all people and all people are you" spread and thank the Kiks.ádi clan of Sheet'ká for granting permission for this use. These five dance robes center around the story of Kaxhatjaa, the Herring Rock Woman, and illustrate our connection to the land and each other. The artist would also like to thank fellow Tlingit artist Alison Bremner for her guidance on formline design during the creation of the art.

REMEMBER

POEM BY U.S. POET LAUREATE JOY HARJO

ILLUSTRATIONS BY CALDECOTT MEDALIST MICHAELA GOADE

RANDOM HOUSE STUDIO ■ NEW YORK

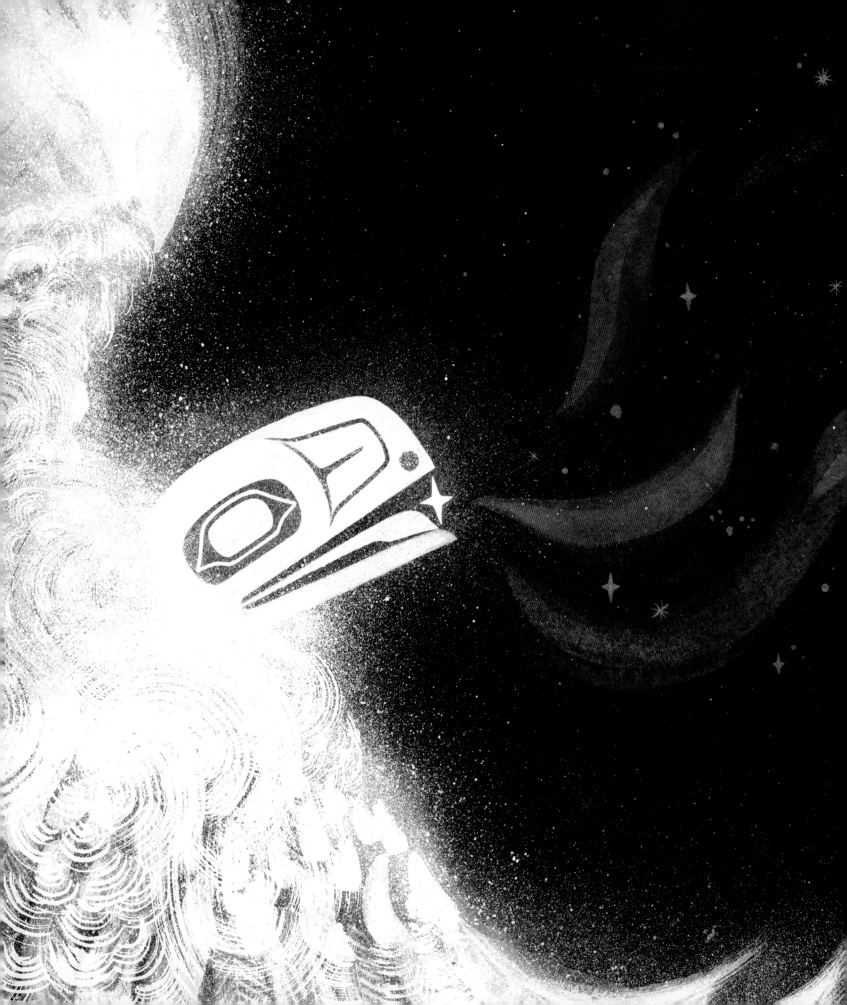

emember the sky that you were born under,
know each of the star's stories.

Remember the moon,
know who she is.

Remember the sun's birth at dawn,
that is the strongest point of time.

Remember sundown and the giving away to night.

Remember your birth, how your mother
struggled to give you form and breath.

You are evidence of her life,
and her mother's, and hers.

Remember your father.
He is your life, also.

Remember the earth whose skin you are:
red earth, black earth, yellow earth,
white earth, brown earth, we are earth.

Remember the plants, trees,
animal life who all have their tribes,
their families, their histories, too.
Talk to them, listen to them.

They are alive poems.

Remember the wind.

Remember her voice.

She knows the origin of this universe.

Remember you are all people and all people are you.

Remember all is in motion,
is growing, is you.

Remember you are this universe.

And this universe is you.

Remember.

WITH GRATITUDE
FOR THOSE WHO TEACH US
HOW TO NAVIGATE
THE CHALLENGING STORY FIELD
WITH GRACE, WILDNESS,
AND HEART —J.H.

AUTHOR'S NOTE

I like to think of a poem as a pocket or an envelope that can hold dreams, thoughts, or anything else that you might put together with words, rhythm, and patterns of lines and sounds. Some poems are written on paper. Some poems are carried around in memory and live in your heart. I like to imagine a poetry room in my heart. The first poems planted there were from my mother. She recited poetry she had learned in her one-room schoolhouse. She also wrote songs that were like poetry with wings. I loved to see her type them out on the typewriter that sat on the kitchen table, then sing them. She wrote what was in her heart. In the poetry room of your imagination, there is space for all the poems that you will ever need.

We need poems when we lose something important to us, when we need to pay attention, or when we need to put something back together that has been broken. In my Mvskoke tradition, we have songs for growing corn, for stopping a storm, and for expressing gratitude for the beauty on this earth. To speak or to sing aloud or on paper is a powerful way to bring your thoughts, your yearnings, the most secret dreams of your heart into existence. "Remember" came into the world to remind me who I am as a human being living on this generous earth. We all need to be reminded to remember. Poetry feeds our hearts and minds so we can walk forward in our story with a renewed spirit. You can write your own poems to carry in your pocket or your notebook. The best place to carry them will always be your heart. There they are always with you.

—JOY HARJO

ARTIST'S NOTE

Joy's poem begins with an invitation to remember the stars, the moon, and the sun. These words reminded me of traditional Tlingit creation stories, ones about Raven and his trickster ways, and of how he first released the stars, the moon, and the sun. In time, Raven brought us other gifts such as fire, rivers, and the tides, eventually forming the world as we know it. But in the beginning, there was night, and then there was day. It felt right that the art should also begin with Raven bringing light to the world.

Further inspiration came from the Tlingit concept of haa shagoon, which is the understanding that our ancestors are united with the present and future generations. I brought this into the artwork by imagining a young Tlingit girl who is called upon to remember where and who she comes from. As she grows, she learns the power that comes from this knowledge.

As I worked on this book, I wanted the pages to feel like a celebration of Lingít Aaní, or Tlingit land. The ocean and rain forest settings reflect our ancestral home in Southeast Alaska, and the animals and plants I included hold special cultural significance. I also hint at traditional stories, as well as referencing traditional dances and regalia. Additionally, in imagery such as the moon, the sun, and certain animals, you'll find elements of formline design, the traditional art style belonging to many of the Indigenous Nations along the Pacific Northwest coast, including the Tlingit. Formline is a unique, complex art form imbued with cultural meaning, history, and protocol; in my eyes it is a true "alive poem."

I hope this book helps you remember where and who you come from. This will mean different things to different people, and that is a beautiful thing. We all have our own important stories to remember and share with the world. I will carry this book in my heart always. I hope you do, too.

Gunalchéesh,

MICHAELA GOADE